SUDDENLY—
A WITCH!

Irene Bowen

SUDDENLY-
A WITCH!

illustrated by
Susan Purdy

J. B. Lippincott Company
Philadelphia   New York

Also by Irene Bowen

THE MYSTERY OF THE TALKING WELL
MYSTERY OF EEL ISLAND
THE STOLEN SPOON MYSTERY

For their kind permission
to reprint material copyrighted by them,
thanks go to Houghton Mifflin Company for the lines
from HOW BLACKSNAKE CAUGHT THE WOLF, *from*
DADDY JAKE THE RUNAWAY AND SHORT STORIES TOLD AFTER DARK,
in THE COMPLETE TALES OF UNCLE REMUS
by Joel Chandler Harris, compiled by
Richard Chase.

FOR ALL MY YOUNG SCHOOL FRIENDS
WHO LOVE HALLOWEEN
·

My thanks to
Deborah Brown of Schenectady, N.Y.
for suggesting the title

CONTENTS

SUDDENLY-
A WITCH!

1
A Pumpkin Trip

When Susan closed her eyes, she could almost believe it was still summer. The air was as soft and warm as it was in August. But everything was quiet; there were no late summer insect sounds and when she opened her eyes she knew that summer was long past. Hardly a leaf was left on the trees, some of the fields were brown now and most of the birds had gone. Fall sometimes made Susan feel sad in a pleasant sort of way, but today she couldn't feel even the least bit sad.

It was almost the end of October. Susan and her mother and her best friend Barbara were going out into the country to look for pumpkins for Halloween. They wanted to find the two biggest pumpkins there were and put them out on their porch roofs. The girls lived across the street from each other and they thought it would be great fun to have two pumpkin faces looking down on the street, one from each side, while their owners were out at a Halloween party.

Susan and Barbara could hardly wait for the party. It would be almost like going to a real haunted house. Becky, one of their friends, had just moved into a big old monster of a place, three stories high, that looked as if the Addams Family could live there very happily. After awhile the upper floors would be made into apartments, but right now no one else was living in the house and it was a wonderful ch   to have a really spooky Halloween party.

Be   invitation had come last week:

On Halloween night at seven o'clock,
Come to my house. Don't bother to knock.
A ghostly guide will meet you there,
And lead you down to his shadowy lair.
You'll see things below that will curl your toes,
You won't escape till the first cock crows.
Wear your costume and your false face,
And be ready for fun all over the place.

Susan loved spooky things. Barbara did, too, but not quite so much. When they went to the library Barbara would take out horse stories or books about girls in school, but Susan always asked the librarian to find her a scary mystery. She'd read almost every one on the shelves. Sometimes the stories were so scary that she didn't dare read them just before bedtime. But it was fun to be scared by a story, just as it was fun to feel sad on top when you were really happy underneath.

She was thinking about how strange this was when Barbara poked her and said, "Look, there's a place that sells pumpkins. Why don't we stop?"

"Oh, we're going to Mrs. Gordon's. Mother called her up and she said she had some huge ones."

"That's where you got Spooky, isn't it?" Barbara asked. "You should dress up like a witch for Becky's party and bring Spooky, too."

"Maybe I will." Susan thought it sounded like a wonderful idea if she could keep track of Spooky all the time they were at the party.

She remembered very well the first time she'd seen Spooky. Mrs. Gordon had called to say there was a new batch of kittens at the farm. Susan and her mother had gone out to see them one Saturday. It was dark in the unused horse stall where the mother cat had her box. At first all they could see was a black shape in one corner—cat and kittens all curled up together. Suddenly a tiny white kitten face seemed to float in the air right toward them.

"O-o-o-h, look at that!"

Mrs. Gordon reached out and picked up the little creature. It was coal black except for face and ears which were white. In the dusky corner of the barn only the face had showed, making it look as if the kitten had no body.

"That was sure spooky," Susan had giggled. "Oh, Mother, can't I please, please have him?"

Of course there was no question about his name. Spooky he had been from the start. The name was a good one for him. He enjoyed hiding in things and under things and popping out at people. On nights when the wind blew and clouds scudded across the sky there was no holding him. He prowled through the house and when Susan let him out, he was away in a flash and sometimes didn't come back till morning. She liked to pretend he was a witch cat and had gone off to ride with the witches.

They drove into the front yard of the Gordon farm. A large collie rushed up to the car, barking and waving a plumy tail. Several boys were practicing with a football; one of them was in the girls' grade at school.

There was a huge orange pile at one side of the house: tall pumpkins, squatty pumpkins, perfect round ones and lopsided ones, tiny ones not much bigger than a large apple, and tremendous ones that could have carried Cinderella to the ball. It was very hard deciding. Should they make big fat round jack-o'-lanterns or tall thin jack-o'-lanterns?

"I think I'll make a sad face on mine," Susan finally said, "so this long skinny one will be just right."

"Well, I'm going to get this fat one then," Barbara decided, "and I'll see whether I want to make a funny face or a scary face."

Susan's mother was getting some winter squash and gourds. She also bought two small pumpkins because her club was coming to the house for a meeting Halloween night and she wanted fall decorations.

"How's your kitty?" Mrs. Gordon asked. "He must be nearly grown up now."

"He's awfully frisky," Susan told her. "Some nights we can't get him in at all."

"Well, watch out on Halloween," said Mrs. Gordon. "He looked to me like a real Halloween cat."

"I think so, too," Susan agreed. "I'll have to keep my eyes on him that night all right."

They loaded the vegetables into the trunk and started back to town. A few minutes later Susan's mother turned off on a narrow dirt road.

"Now where are we going?"

"This is still the Gordons' land and Mrs. Gordon said there's nice bittersweet growing along here. I'd like some for my party. There it is, next to that old stone wall. Get those clippers out of the glove compartment, will you, Susan?"

A smell of dry leaves was in the air, and once in awhile a whiff of smoke from somebody's bonfire. The girls started fooling around, chasing each other in circles in the road and balancing on the stone wall. Susan grew so warm she took her jacket off and let the breeze cool her. The wind was stronger on top of this hill than down in the village. Up here they could see the whole valley across to the hills on the other side.

"Oh, wouldn't it be fun to live here!" Susan cried.

"Not in the winter," said her mother very firmly.

"Yes, it would. I'd love to have the snow piled way up and the road closed so the school bus couldn't come after me."

"Not me," said Barbara. "I'd rather live in town where everybody is."

On the way down the long hill they left the car windows open and breathed in all the lovely autumn smells. "Look out your head doesn't fall off," giggled Barbara. "You look just like a puppy dog hanging out of the window."

"Come over right after supper and we'll fix our jack-o'-lanterns," Susan reminded her as they jumped out of the car back home.

2
Halloween Is Coming!

Barbara arrived before the dishes were done. The girls spread newspapers on the kitchen floor and Susan's father brought in the big heavy pumpkins.

"For heaven's sake, be careful with those knives," Susan's mother warned anxiously. "One slip and we'd be going around hunting for lost fingers in dark corners. Call us to help when you come to the hard parts."

"We will," they promised, only half listening.

"Let's draw the faces first," Susan said. "Then we can change them if we need to."

"I'm going to cut the top off and dig out the seeds before I start the face," Barbara decided.

"Do you save the seeds and toast them?"

"No. I don't think they taste that great," said Barbara. "I remember we did it in first grade. Oh, darn," she sputtered. "I always have trouble fitting the top back on again."

"My mother showed me what to do about that," Susan told her. "You cut a little piece out, not all the way through, just the orange skin part, and you make the cut right across the edge of the cover. Then when you put the cover on, match the two parts of the cut and the cover fits."

"Hey, that's neat. Your mother's smart."

"Well, thank you," said Susan's mother coming in. "How are you doing?"

"All right. Is this a good face?" Susan had just drawn it in.

"I think you should make everything bigger and farther apart," her mother advised. "Remember, you want him to show from the porch roof."

"Holy Toledo, I made mine cross-eyed!" Barbara exploded.

"Don't worry about it. He looks good that way."

There was silence for a few minutes while they both put the finishing touches on their pumpkin faces. Outside the wind was rising. Suddenly Spooky danced into the kitchen sideways, his tail straight up and bristling.

"Look at him," Barbara laughed. "He knows his special day is coming."

"Oh, he always acts this way when the wind blows," Susan said. "Should I let him out, Mother?"

"Well, he'll be wild if you don't. And he'll be wild if you do, too. You probably won't be able to get him back in tonight."

Susan opened the door and Spooky shot through it like a small black rocket. Susan went out on the porch. The wind was roaring through the trees and leaves were blowing all over the yard. Branches waved in front of the street light, throwing weird shadows. All at once Susan felt wild, too. She ran down into the yard and turned somersaults in the leaves. Spooky pounced out at her from a clump of bushes. Barbara jumped off the porch and they began tossing leaves at each other and shrieking with laughter.

"Girls, girls," Susan's mother was calling from the porch. "Come back here. You haven't even got sweaters on and it's getting cold."

Slowly, out of breath, they trailed back into the kitchen and started to clean up the pumpkin mess. They each had a glass of cider and then it was time for Barbara to go home. Tomorrow was another school day. Susan's father went with her to carry the heavy jack-o'-lantern.

"We'll put them out tomorrow night," the girls told each other. "The night before Halloween."

Later when Susan's mother came in to say good night, she found Susan sitting on the windowsill looking out. All up and down the street, lights were on in other upstairs windows. Other children were getting ready for bed. A few houses already had jack-o'-lanterns glowing in windows or by front doors. Two boys in the house next to Barbara's had made a tall ghost in their yard. It had a pumpkin head with a flashlight inside. Somewhere out there in all the Halloween eeriness, Spooky frisked around, perhaps meeting other witch cats, perhaps already broomstick-riding.

"Oh, I love Halloween best of all!"

Her mother laughed. "Yes, I know. And then when Christmas comes, that's the time you love best. And in the spring when everything's beginning, that's your favorite time. Well, I'm like that, too. Hop into bed now. Goodness, are you sitting here in just your pajamas with the window open?"

Susan was so keyed up it took her a little while to get sleepy, but finally she felt herself drifting off. The last things she heard were the gusty wind and, faintly, a cat meowing.

3
Bad Luck

Susan woke up in the night with a very unpleasant feeling. "Oh, no!" she thought. "This *can't* be true!" But it was. A scratchy feeling deep down in her throat hurt more than just a tickle and made her want to swallow over and over. The really bad chest colds always started this way.

She went into the bathroom for a drink of water and still seemed to hear a cat crying somewhere. Maybe Spooky wanted to come in. She tiptoed downstairs and looked out the back door. The wind had quieted down. In a corner of the porch stood a tall black shape—the jack-o'-lantern. A smaller black something near it moved toward the door. There was another plaintive meow.

Susan opened the door and Spooky trotted in, acting as if it was only to be expected—people waiting on him in the middle of the night. He dashed upstairs ahead of her and when she climbed back into bed he burrowed under the covers and curled up way down by her feet. It was nice to have him there but she wondered how he could breathe.

The drink of water hadn't done much good. Her throat was still scratchy and she slept only off and on for the rest of the night. Then when it was nearly morning she fell asleep so soundly that her mother had to wake her up.

By this time the tickle was down around her larynx and it made her cough to say anything. She tried to speak but only a whisper came out. And then the horribleness of the whole thing was too much and she began to cry.

"Oh, Susie!" Her mother sat down on the bed and put her arms around Susan. "What a shame. You probably got chilled yesterday running around so much without your coat. Maybe that didn't make any difference. Who knows about these bugs anyway? Now hop out of bed for a few minutes and let me smooth out the sheets. Go and wash your face and hands and make a quick pass at your teeth." She began to laugh. "Here, what's this mysterious lump at the foot of the bed? It's rather large for a bedbug, but it does seem to be alive."

Susan almost giggled but it hurt too much. Mother pulled the sheets all the way back and Spooky stood up, yawned, stretched, and jumped off the bed. He left the room in a dignified manner, his tail straight up in the air.

A little while later Susan was back in bed propped up on a couple of pillows. The vaporizer bubbled away close beside her, filling the room with a rather pleasant smell.

Footsteps sounded outside and her father came in with a tray. "Well," he said, "I hear you've got the epizootic."

Any other time Susan would have laughed because the epizootic was something horses had and besides, it sounded so silly, but today she couldn't. Two tears rolled down her cheeks.

"Now have some breakfast and try to go to sleep again," her father said. "We'll call the doctor as soon as he's in his office and get you some of that stuff that worked last time. We'll lick this bug yet." He helped her arrange the pillows and put the tray across her knees.

There was a tiny sprig of bittersweet in a doll's pitcher on the tray. Her mother had cut an orange into slices and the toast into strips the way she liked. Cocoa was in a small gold and white pot—part of her grandmother's little-girl tea set. One of the cups in the set was there, too, and an old-fashioned spoon with a maple leaf handle which said "Souvenir of Canada." Being sick was almost fun when the tray looked so pretty.

She was just finishing as the front door opened downstairs. "Susan, hurry up, we're late," Barbara called. All her misery came rushing back. She couldn't even squeak loud enough for Barbara to hear. There were footsteps below and a low-voiced conversation. Then Barbara called, "I'm sorry you're sick. I'll bring your homework tonight," and the door banged shut.

It was a long long day. Much of the time Susan dozed and the vaporizer bubbled. Spooky seemed to know she didn't feel good and spent a large part of the day curled up by her feet. Mother fixed another fancy tray at lunch time with jellied consomme, thin slices of bread and butter, cut-up fruit, and a chocolate milkshake. She read aloud while Susan was eating. It was the story about Winnie the Pooh getting caught in the Heffalump trap.

Late in the afternoon after it was quite dark, her father came in. "There's a big pumpkin head downstairs that wants to go out on the porch roof so he can see his friend across the street."

"Oh!" Susan croaked, sitting up in bed. "Does Barbara have her jack-o'-lantern out? She never even stopped in like she said she would."

"Yes, she did." Mother came in with a tall glass of juice. "You were asleep and besides, I don't want her catching your cold. Let's wait till Daddy gets your jack-o'-lantern out and then we can go look at it through the front-room window and you'll be able to see Barbara's, too."

Her father brought in the jack-o'-lantern, lighted, for her to see before he climbed out on the flat roof and set it near, but not too near the edge. The mournful face she had

carved glowed eerily in the dusky room. A few minutes later, she and her mother looked past it across the street to another pumpkin face on Barbara's roof.

"He looks funny cross-eyed," Susan giggled and then started to cough.

"Come on now, back to bed," said her mother. "You can get up and look at them again later."

It wasn't till after supper that she thought to ask if Barbara had brought any homework.

"A few math problems and a chapter to read in your social studies book. But you aren't doing any homework tonight. I'll get you some clean pajamas and change the sheets on your bed and then I want you to rest some more."

It seemed as if she had been sleeping all day, but the sheets felt cool and clean, and she didn't really want to do anything else. "Did Barbara say anything about the party?" she whispered.

"No, dear," her mother answered. By this time Susan knew that she wouldn't possibly be able to go. A large tear squeezed out of the corner of each eye and slid down into her hair. She thought of a silly song, "I have tears in my ears lying on my back in bed crying over you," but somehow even that didn't make her feel like laughing. Mother hugged her.

"I'm as sorry as I can be about the party, but there will be other parties, you know."

"Not in a haunted house," Susan squeaked.

"Well, you can't really be sure about that."

Susan looked at her mother in disgust. She did hate being told impossibilities just to comfort her.

Her mother began to laugh. "All right, since you're so annoyed at me, I suppose it was a silly thing to say. Probably there won't be another party in a haunted house very soon. Anyway, that isn't the point. I know how disappointing it is for you, and Daddy and I are disappointed, too. But things like this happen to us all, and if you start feeling sorry for yourself, you'll melt away into a puddle of tears. I'd rather have a little girl than a saltwater pool."

4
Halloween Inside

By the next morning a lot of the tightness had gone from Susan's chest, but every time she coughed she rattled, and when she took a deep breath there was a sort of creaking deep down inside. "You sound like a rusty hinge," her mother said as she brought the breakfast tray. This morning the orange was cut to look like a small jack-o'-lantern.

Outside it was cloudy with little spurts of rain. The bedroom looked warm and cheerful and Susan would have been glad just to be lying there resting except for the party. But she knew there wasn't any more use talking about that.

Suddenly she remembered her mother's party. "Are the ladies still coming tonight?" she asked.

"Yes, of course."

"But what if I get worse or something?"

"Why, you won't get worse. You're better now than you were last night. And Daddy will be right here if you need him."

Susan looked so forlorn that her mother went on, "You could do something to help me. You know those two little pumpkins we bought the other day? If you'll make a face on each one, I'll use them as part of my centerpiece. Use magic markers instead of cutting them out; it's easier and the pumpkins last better."

Susan had to make several sketches before she came up with faces that were right. One face had a foolish lopsided grin and the other one was sad with droopy eyes and a turned-down mouth. Between eating and resting, she'd taken most all day on them. By the time they were done, early darkness was beginning to close down. When her father came home, he lit the candle in the porch-roof jack-o'-lantern and also brought in a small one somebody in the office had made. Spooky looked at it with suspicion and walked all around it on top of the bureau where it sat grinning cheerfully in the dusk.

The supper tray was not as fancy tonight because Mother was getting ready for her guests. But there was a Halloween cupcake Susan's teacher had sent home with Barbara. And just as she was finishing, Barbara came to the door again. She asked if Susan would like to see her costume.

Susan almost said no; then she remembered what her mother had said about feeling sorry for herself. Besides, she was curious.

Barbara was dressed as an owl. Her mother had taken a plain eye mask and decorated it with earlike tufts sticking up, and had made the eyes huge and scary. Barbara had on a long cape made of some kind of soft black cloth all cut into fringes and floating bits. She really looked good. "I'll come over tomorrow and tell you all about the party," she promised, "and maybe bring you something. Becky said to tell you she's sorry you can't come."

After she'd gone, Susan had rather a struggle to keep from crying for a few minutes. Then the doorbell rang again. It was not trick-or-treaters as she expected, but her mother's first party guest, Miss Wilkins, the village librarian. Mother had worked for her a long time ago and they were special friends. She was Susan's special friend, too, so she came right upstairs.

Miss Wilkins didn't spend any time making polite remarks. "How dreadful!" she sputtered. "Here's this poor child cooped up without a thing in the world to read!" It sounded as if she were scolding Susan's mother.

Mother didn't look very much upset. "I know it," she said, "but she hasn't felt very much like reading the last couple of days. Anyway, I'll bet you've got something to help the situation."

Miss Wilkins looked disgusted. She was not fond of expressions like "I'll bet," which she said people didn't really mean. She rummaged in her large needlepoint bag, reminding Susan, as she did in many ways, of Mary Poppins. "This came today," she announced, pulling out a fat book. "Just the thing for Halloween." It was a new collection of ghost and witch stories.

"Oh, thank you," Susan whispered. "Daddy can read it to me tonight."

"I hope he does," Miss Wilkins said decidedly. "It must be very disappointing for you to miss Becky's party. I know. I had the mumps for Halloween when I was a little girl and I was going to have a party myself."

Susan stared at her. Somehow she just couldn't imagine Miss Wilkins as a little girl or having the mumps. Miss Wilkins looked as if she knew what Susan was thinking, which made Susan feel rather silly. To her relief, Spooky walked in waving his tail, and hopped up on the bed.

"Now there's a real Halloween cat," Miss Wilkins remarked.

Susan told her how Spooky came by his name.

"I can see he's something out of the ordinary, perhaps even capable of magic."

"Magic?"

"You know, people used to think cats had supernatural powers. Of course we don't believe anything like that now, but he is a black cat, and it is Halloween, and, well, who knows?"

"Now come on downstairs and don't give the child any more ideas than she already has," said Mother as the door-bell rang again. "I suspect she thinks Spooky is a witch's cat anyway."

How had her mother known that, Susan wondered after they had gone. And did Miss Wilkins really think he might be magic or was she only pretending? You couldn't always tell with grown-ups, especially someone who reminded you of Mary Poppins.

Her father read three ghost stories and brought in a glass of juice. Then she got ready for bed, had a last look at the two jack-o'-lanterns outside, and slipped between the sheets. The vaporizer began to bubble-bubble-bubble very softly.

Spooky had left during the stories. "Out with the witches by now," Susan thought. "Even if he is magic, it isn't doing me any good. Come on, Spooky," she whispered. "Make some Halloween magic for me."

She waited, but nothing happened. The room was quiet and dark. Though the door was closed, faintly the sound of laughing and talking floated up from downstairs. Once in awhile there were shouts and running feet outdoors as trick-or-treaters went around.

Susan wasn't really sleepy. But it was very warm and comfortable in bed and her throat hardly hurt at all. The vaporizer must be helping. She turned her head to look at it. "Bubble-bubble-bubble—"

"Maybe it's a witch's kettle bubbling away," she thought. "Maybe it's magic, too, on Halloween, like Spooky."

The vaporizer suddenly bubbled faster and a big cloud of steam poured out of the spout. Susan took a deep breath. She felt almost dizzy and closed her eyes for a moment.

When she opened them again, there was Spooky sitting on the windowsill looking at her.

5

Halloween Outside

Susan sat straight up in bed and stared. How did Spooky get there? He couldn't have come from outside; it was much too far to the ground. And her father had closed the bedroom door. She looked around; yes, it was still closed.

Spooky jumped down and stalked across to Susan's bed. He stood looking up at her. She'd never seen his eyes so green. They glowed at her like two little lights. His white face looked spookier than ever.

"Mer-r-row!" he said loudly.

"What do you want?" Susan asked.

"Mer-r-r-row!" he said again, even more loudly. The tip

of his tail twitched. Then he turned and walked back toward the window. He looked around and meowed once more.

Susan slid out of bed and followed him, since that seemed to be what he expected. He hopped up on the windowsill again. There was no screen and the storm window was not yet on. She looked out and nearly jumped out of her skin. There, just beyond the windowsill, bobbing around in the air for all the world like a boat tied to a dock, was a broom. A plain rather shabby old broom, floating flat out.

"A broomstick!" breathed Susan, not quite believing, yet believing. After all, this was Halloween, and she'd always thought Spooky was a witch cat.

But where was the witch? Here was a witch's broomstick and a witch's cat but no witch.

Spooky was fairly dancing up and down on the window-sill making little pr-r-rps and meows. Suddenly he gave a leap and landed on the straw part of the broom. It wobbled a little but stayed up in the air. A very strange idea came to Susan. Perhaps she was supposed to ride the broomstick herself. She wasn't really a witch, but Spooky was her cat and she had planned to be a witch at Becky's party.

Cautiously she sat on the windowsill and swung her legs outside. The broomstick was very close. Spooky kept telling her to come in cat language. She slid out of the window and straddled the broomstick, holding on with both hands.

"Now what?" she thought. "How do I make it go any-where? Move!" she said, almost without thinking.

The broomstick obligingly floated forward a few feet, then stopped by the corner of the house. Susan could see her sad-faced jack-o'-lantern staring out from the porch roof. "Take me over closer," she commanded, and at once the broomstick moved through the air.

"Oh, this is fun!" she cried. "I love being a witch!"

"Well, you'd better know the rules or you'll be in trouble before long," said a gloomy voice.

"My goodness, you can talk!" gasped Susan.

"Naturally. What do you think my mouth is for?" returned the jack-o'-lantern rather crossly.

"What do you mean, know the rules?" Susan asked, feel-ing shy. It seemed so odd to be talking to a jack-o'-lantern she had made herself.

"Magic is not something to fool around with or use lightly," the jack-o'-lantern stated firmly. "Too many peo-ple waste it. Look at those fellows who have three wishes.

They use one to see if it really works. Then they wish for some silly thing with the second one, and finally they use the third one to get rid of the silly thing."

"But what are the rules?" Susan asked again. She had a feeling that the jack-o'-lantern liked to talk and would go on and on if she didn't interrupt.

"You are only a witch while you have your broomstick," he told her solemnly. "If you are riding on it or holding it, you're all right, but the minute you let go of it, watch out!"

"What will happen?" Susan asked anxiously.

"Just don't do it," the jack-o'-lantern said. "But you probably will," he added mournfully. "Young girls don't have any sense. Only don't say I didn't warn you!"

"Oh, for heaven's sake!" snapped Susan. "I'm going over and talk to Barbara's jack-o'-lantern. He's probably not such a sourpuss." And off she rode, forgetting that she was the one who had carved him into a sourpuss in the first place.

On Barbara's porch roof her jack-o'-lantern grinned cheerfully into the dark. He certainly was cross-eyed, but that didn't make him look any less happy.

"Hello, my bewitching young friend!" he called. "Glad to see you out enjoying Halloween. How do you like broomstick riding?"

"I love it," she told him, "but what did *he* mean"—she looked across to her own house—"about not letting go of my broomstick?"

"Keep a good tight grip on it and you'll be all right," said the cheerful jack-o'-lantern, not really telling her any more than the sad one had done.

"Are there some other rules?" she asked, hoping there weren't.

"Use your head. That's all; use your head," chuckled the jack-o'-lantern. Susan could see why he thought this was important; he was all head.

"Do I just tell the broomstick where to go?" she wanted to know next. "That's what I've been doing. Or could I steer it with my hands?"

"Try it out. Try it out," her smiling friend urged. "Don't be timid. Witches are never timid."

Susan pulled on the handle with her left hand and the broomstick obediently turned left. A pull with her right hand turned her the other way. "Guess I'll try going up," she said, and leaned back hard. The broomstick pointed straight up, then made two complete somersaults like an airplane doing stunts.

"Stop!" yelled Susan as it came around the second time. The jack-o'-lantern roared with laughter. "I knew she'd do some foolish thing!" came a gloomy voice from across the street.

"Mer-r-r-row!" snarled Spooky with his claws still fastened tightly into the broom.

"Whew!" Susan gasped. "Why didn't you tell me it would do that?"

"Now you know you can do tricks if you want to," chuckled the jack-o'-lantern. "With practice you'll be a real loop-the-loop artist."

"If I only looked like a witch," Susan said sadly. "Who ever heard of a witch in polka-dot pajamas?"

"Don't worry about that. For tonight you are a witch whether you're dressed like one or not. Besides, what do you care? Nobody can see you as long as you're holding on to your broomstick."

"My goodness! You mean I'm invisible?"

"Certainly. That's part of your magic, too."

"Oh, boy! I know what. I'm going over to Becky's and haunt the party—I mean—can witches *haunt* things? Maybe only ghosts can do that."

"Go right ahead. Whether it's haunting or bewitching, it will stir up the party all right."

"Hold on tight, Spooky. Here we go! Good-bye, Happy Pumpkin!" They swooped across the street, diving under the telephone wires. "Good-bye, Sad Pumpkin! I'm sorry I called you a sourpuss."

"Watch out for TV antennas. And don't forget—a witch's best friend is her cat!" the voice of the sad jack-o'-lantern floated after her as she sailed up over the treetops.

6

The Bewitched Party

Clouds which had covered the sky all day were breaking up now and drifting across the moon. For the first time Susan wondered why she didn't feel cold. Here she was in nothing but pajamas flying around through the air on a late fall night and not even a goose pimple. The chest cold that had spoiled—nearly spoiled—her Halloween, seemed to be all gone now. "Must be the magic," she thought.

From below came the sound of the town clock striking seven thirty. It was not as late as she'd thought with so many exciting things happening. People must still be arriving at Becky's party. "Come on, broomstick. To Becky's house," she ordered.

She was learning to control the broomstick better now. On her way she swooped down where groups of children were going from house to house along the street. Once she cackled with what she hoped was witchlike laughter and left them staring all around trying to find where the sound

came from. Then she knocked the tall hat from the head of a make-believe witch. It was a girl in the fifth grade who sometimes made fun of her. The witch ran after her hat, picked it out of a puddle and began to argue with her friends because she was sure they had knocked it off.

But Susan couldn't waste any more time fooling around. She flew over the school and across the park and there was Becky's house below her.

It was a wonderful Halloween house. Painted dark green, it had a circular part at one corner that looked like a tower. Inside, of course, was a round room on each of the three floors. Becky was trying to persuade her mother to let her have one of them for her own room. There was an iron fence with a gate in front, although Becky's father was planning to have it taken down.

Some children in costume came up to the gate. Susan floated down on her broomstick and perched on the fence to watch. Spooky yawned and stretched and started to wash his face.

A clump of bushes grew right inside. From behind it stepped a skeleton, the "ghostly guide" of the invitation. He beckoned. Timidly the children pushed open the gate. Someone gave a squeal of fright as a ghost rose up, as if from nowhere, a little way from the sidewalk. The gate creaked shut again and the ghost disappeared.

The skeleton led the way up the front walk. Susan hopped down and went over to the gate, being careful not to let go of her broom. She looked closely and saw a piece of plastic picture wire tied to the top of the tall iron gate. In the dark she couldn't see where it led, but when she pushed the gate open, the ghost rose up from under the branch of a nearby tree. So that's how it worked! The wire ran from the gate over the tree branch and when the gate was moved the ghost went up and down.

"Hey!" yelled the skeleton in the voice of Becky's older brother, "That gate moved by itself!" He started back down the walk. The other children, thinking this was part of the fun, watched for a minute, then went on around the house, following signs which pointed toward the back.

Susan closed the gate. Becky's brother stopped and stared, then came on very slowly. He reached the gate and pushed it back and forth. Susan didn't make a sound but all at once Spooky meowed. The boy jumped and looked all around, but Spooky, too, was invisible because of witch magic.

"Something's goofy," muttered the skeleton uneasily, but just then more guests came along so he stepped behind the bushes to be ready for them. Susan followed the first group of children around the side of the house.

Becky's house had an outside cellar door. This was the way the party guests went in. There were stone steps going down and at the foot of the steps a doorway. A blue light shone from inside the door and across the entrance was draped a huge spider web with a plastic spider in it. Each person had to push this aside to get in. There wasn't anyone right at the door, so when the others were inside, Susan pushed her way in after them.

The cellar was big and old-fashioned like the rest of the house and had several rooms. At the foot of the stairs there had once been a laundry. Susan tiptoed past big washtubs, holding tightly to her broom with Spooky perched on her shoulder. Another blue light was fastened over the door into the next room. Just inside, someone reached out an arm in a hairy monster glove, beckoning anyone who came along. As Susan started through the door, the arm shot out and poked Spooky who let out a snarl. The monster, Becky's younger sister, gave a gasp of fright because she could hear a cat right in front of her but could see nothing. Susan slipped through the doorway very quietly.

She was in the main room of the cellar now. Masks were fastened here and there on the walls with flashlights either inside or underneath to make them look even more scary. Cardboard skeletons, ghosts, witches, and cats hung from the ceiling, some decorated with luminous paint which glowed eerily in the gloom. At the opposite end of the room was another door. Every time anyone came near it, a ghost jumped out and made a grab. The room was full of children laughing, squealing, and pretending to be scared. Susan backed into a corner so no one else would bump into her. She watched the guests go all around and finally start upstairs to the kitchen above.

Suddenly something moved in the shadows under the stairs and there was a deep groan. Children on the stairs screamed and ran up as fast as they could. Susan tiptoed along by the wall to see. A figure was sitting on a low chair all wrapped up in a dark coat or cape. Long gray hair hung down over its face. Then Susan saw the cello and knew this must be Becky's older sister who played in the high school orchestra. She was really pretty good, but you'd never know it now by the horrible groans that came from the cello. Every so often she'd throw her head back, shake the

gray wig, and give a lunatic laugh.

By this time a good many children had come through the cellar and gone upstairs. The skeleton appeared from outside and said, "I guess that's everybody. I was counting and I don't think anybody else is supposed to come."

The mad cello player stood up and the ghost and monster came out from their hiding places.

"The craziest thing happened out there," said the skeleton, and told about the moving gate. "It was like something invisible coming in."

Becky's younger sister pulled off her monster glove and said, "Something goofy happened in here, too. I thought there was a cat meowing right in front of me but there wasn't anything there. I even touched something, I know."

"Oh, you're nuttier than I look," the cello player told them. "You've got ghosts on the brain. Let's go up and have something to eat." She leaned her cello against the wall and they all left, still arguing.

Susan waited a minute, then went over and listened at the foot of the stairs. She heard voices right above. Everybody must be in the kitchen. Here was a chance to scare them all. She picked up the cello bow and dragged it across the strings. Hideous sounds came forth. There was sudden silence above. She made another horrible screech.

"W-who's there?" quavered a voice at the top of the stairs. Susan laughed out loud.

"Who are you?" asked another voice, and she realized with horror that she had let go of her broomstick to play the cello. *They could see her!* She snatched it up again as the cello slipped and clattered to the floor.

"What's going on down there?" Becky's father appeared and switched on the cellar light.

"I'm sure I saw someone, but there's nobody there now."

"Somebody *was* playing the cello. Look, it's lying on the floor."

"I told you something funny was going on."

Susan shrank against the wall and held perfectly still as Becky's father came down the cellar stairs and looked all around. "Nobody here now," he announced, and she could hardly keep from giggling. He shut and locked the outside door, then went back up, turning off the light and closing the door behind him.

Susan sat down on the bottom step and rested her chin in her hands. Now what? Did anyone believe yet that a real witch had come to the party?

All at once she straightened up. Of course they didn't. Why should they, when all she had done was what any ordinary person would do, and people had only been fooled because they couldn't see her. Of course it was magic, but a real witch should be able to work more magic than that. She should be casting spells and enchanting things. She didn't know just how to go about this, but it was worth a try.

"Come on, Spooky," she called, but Spooky was more interested in a corner of the old potato bin where there might be a mouse. So Susan started up the stairs by herself.

7

Spooky's Secret

At the top of the stairs she stopped to listen. People were laughing and talking on the other side of the door. How could she sneak into the kitchen without their seeing the door move? Wait a minute. Why not cast a spell to make all the lights go out? Then no one would see the door move.

She tried to think of some magic words. "Abracadabra" sounded silly; everybody said that. But there *was* something from an old book of her mother's. It had worked magic in the story; perhaps it would work magic here, too. She drew a long breath and said softly:

"Watsilla, watsilla
Consario wo!
"Watsilla, watsilla
Consario wo!

LIGHTS OUT!!"

Everything went pitch black. Susan slipped through the door. "Hey! Who blew all the fuses?" someone yelled.

"Wait a minute. Here's a flashlight." As Becky's mother came from the dining room with the light in her hand, Susan pointed her finger at it. "Watsilla, watsilla—" Before she could say any more, the flashlight began to shoot blue sparks.

"Look out! It's got a short!" Down went the flashlight and in the confusion Susan managed to run through the kitchen and dining room and into the living room.

Bright moonlight outside helped her to see. Most of the furniture had been moved out and it looked as though the rest of the party would be in this room. Against one wall stood a huge desk with a cupboard top. What a wonderful place to sit and watch. It would be easy to cast spells from up there. A word to her broomstick and up she went.

"Guess they've been in the dark long enough," she said to herself and repeated her magic words. The lights glowed blue for a moment and then came on again. Becky ran into the room. Susan hadn't seen her before, and recognized her now by her long braids even though she had on a mask and a very good witch costume. Susan looked down at her own wrinkled pajamas and was glad to be invisible.

The rest of the children began to come in from the dining room. They were talking about a power failure. Susan was disgusted. Nobody believed yet that a real witch was here. She'd have to cast some spells that could not be explained in any ordinary way.

The room was really two rooms with a big double doorway between. A brass curtain rod ran across this doorway and apples were hanging from it on strings. In one corner of the room a piece of plastic was spread on the floor. On it was a pan full of water with apples bobbing about. A large tailless black cat was pinned to one wall.

"If you can eat an apple off the string and not touch it with your hands, you get a prize," Becky explained, though of course nearly everybody knew this. "If you can fish an apple out of the pan with your teeth and not use your hands, you get a prize. And there's a first, second, and third prize for pinning the tail on the black cat."

Susan waited and watched while the children divided themselves into three groups. The ones lined up in front of apples on strings were closest. She pointed at the apples and whispered her incantation, not at all sure what kind of spell she was casting. The apples began to spin, slowly, then faster and faster on the ends of their strings. The children stood and stared at them. Someone reached out, but the apples swung away out of reach. No one could touch them.

"Look at the apples!"

"They act like they're bewitched!"

"Something funny *is* going on!"

There was a shriek from the corner where people were bobbing for apples. Susan had sent her witching power in that direction and every apple in the pan was jumping around. Water splashed over everybody and Susan started

to laugh. She laughed so hard she shook, and the broomstick slipped from her hand, toppled off the desk, and hit the floor with a clatter.

She stopped laughing and shrank back against the wall. Would anybody look up and see her perched there on top of the desk? She was sure they would. They must have heard the broom fall. Desperately she whispered, "Watsilla, watsilla, consario wo! Watsilla, watsilla, consario wo! Lights out!" but nothing happened. "Oh, dear, of course it won't work now. I'm not magic or invisible either, without my broomstick. Whatever will I do?" she wondered.

The desk stood next to a door opening into the front entrance hall. If only she could climb down quickly enough, maybe she'd be able to grab her broomstick and get out into this hall before anyone saw who she was. It was worth a try. The desk was tall, but if she slid over the edge and reached down with her feet, the drop wouldn't be so far.

Carefully she inched along and hung her feet over. Down, down she stretched. . . .

"O-oh look! There's somebody up on the desk. Who is it? She's all dressed up in pajamas!"

Susan put one arm over her face and dropped to the floor. Wildly she looked around for the broomstick. She couldn't reach it. Through the door she rushed into the huge shadowy hall. Wide stairs curved upward to the dark second floor. She could hear the children coming after her so up she dashed two at a time.

At the top was a long corridor. She ran down it and found another staircase at the end. Perhaps she could hide somewhere up above.

These stairs led right into the round tower room on the third floor. There were no shades in the windows and the room was bright with moonlight. It was cold, too, because one window was open. Susan tiptoed across the floor and leaned out. What a long way she was from the ground! Looking down almost made her dizzy.

As she turned back from the window, something gleamed on the dusty floor. It was a big safety pin. One of her mother's sayings came to her:

"See a pin and pick it up;
All the day you'll have good luck.
See a pin and let it lie;
All day good luck will pass you by."

Hastily she snatched up the pin. The day was almost over, but she certainly needed good luck now. She fastened the pin to her pajama pocket.

Then she heard voices. They sounded quite close. The children must be coming up here. Where could she hide? There was no furniture in this room, only a lot of boxes. Maybe if she piled them up—But what good would that do? Even if nobody found her, she'd still have to get out of the house and back home somehow. What a mess! The sad jack-o'-lantern had said she'd probably get into trouble and he was right.

He'd said something else, though. If only she could remember. Oh, yes, just as she was flying away, he'd called out, "Don't forget. A witch's best friend is her cat."

"Oh, Spooky! Where are you?" Susan whispered in despair.

"Mer-r-row!" answered Spooky, prancing into the room with his tail in the air.

"Spooky!" She could have hugged him, she was so glad. But he wasn't interested in hugging. He danced across the room to the open window, talking all the way.

Susan followed him. What was he trying to tell her? He was acting exactly the way he had back in her bedroom when all the magic began. Could it possibly mean now what it had meant then?

She leaned out of the window. Yes, the broomstick was there, gently bobbing in the air. How could it be up here when she'd lost it downstairs in the living room? Well, never mind. She didn't know how it had come to be outside her bedroom window either. It was her magic broom and it was here and that was all that mattered.

She swung her leg over the windowsill just as the children reached the top of the stairs and came pouring into the room.

"Look, look! It's the kid in pajamas! She's climbing out of the window! There's a black cat, too!"

"What do you mean? I don't see anybody." For Susan had mounted her broomstick and become invisible again. Spooky jumped and came down on the broom handle right behind her. He scrambled to keep from falling off and she reached a hand back to steady him. He finally reached the broom itself where he could dig his claws in tightly, but not before one of those claws had given Susan a long scratch across the back of her hand.

"Ouch!" she cried, but couldn't stop to worry about a scratch. She was still close to the house and the children were right there in the window. She took a deep breath, gave a bloodcurdling screech and pulled back on the broomstick. They went up into the air, swung around, and flew in front of the window several more times, with Susan giving maniac laughs and gurgles. Finally with a last howl, she rose over the treetops, leaving the children looking everywhere for something they could hear but not see. As she flew off, she heard one of them say, "It was a real witch. I know it was!"

Flying along more slowly above the trees, Susan began to have the feeling her adventure was over. She had a sudden longing to be home again, and comfortable in bed. The scratch on her hand smarted and she felt very tired.

"I'd like to go home now, please, broomstick," she said. "I'm so sleepy!" She gave a tremendous yawn and felt her hands slipping on the broom handle. "Oh, my goodness," she thought. "I can't go to sleep now. I'll fall off. Hurry up, broomstick. I need to get home to bed."

There was a great rush of air. Lights flew by. For a moment she saw two glowing faces, one happy, one sad. "I had a lovely time!" she called, and thought she heard two voices answer, "Happy Hallowe-e-en!"

But her eyes were closing again and the voices seemed very far away. Then they were lost in a much nearer sound— "Bubble, bubble, bubble."

She opened her eyes. She was not on the broomstick any longer. She was in her own bed, and the vaporizer was bubbling beside her.

She lay there thinking, "I don't remember landing on my windowsill or coming in or getting in bed." And then the thought came over her like a wave, "It was all a dream!"

"Oh, no," she said out loud. "It *couldn't* have been a dream. It *must* have happened. I can't bear it to be a dream!"

But she was lying in bed, and the vaporizer was bubbling, and she could hear the voices of her mother's guests through her closed bedroom door. It was all just as it had been when the whole thing started.

Something bumped softly against her foot. She sat up. Spooky was on the bed, gazing at her with green mysterious eyes, the tip of his tail barely twitching. And her door *was* closed. Had someone let him in while she'd been asleep?

Then she noticed an uncomfortable feeling. She pulled her hand out from under the bedclothes and looked at it. In the dim light she could see a long scratch across the back. It was a new scratch. It smarted and there were a few drops of dried blood on it.

Her hand touched her pajama pocket and felt the cool metal of the big safety pin which had not been there before. She looked at Spooky. "It *was* real, wasn't it?"

But Spooky only winked one eye and twitched his tail.